THE KNIGHTS OF THE BLACK EARTH

THE KNIGHTS
OF THE
BLACK EARTH
*Margaret Weis
and Don Perrin*

VICTOR GOLLANCZ
LONDON

First published in Great Britain 1995
by Victor Gollancz
An imprint of the Cassell Group
Wellington House, 125 Strand, London WC2R 0BB

First published in the United States 1995
by Penguin Books USA Inc.

A catalogue record for this book is
available from the British Library.

ISBN 0 575 06060 3

Typeset in Great Britain by
CentraCet Ltd, Cambridge
Printed and bound in Great Britain
by Mackays of Chatham plc, Chatham, Kent

This book is lovingly dedicated to:
Bayne and Elizabeth Perrin
and
Donald Bayne Perrin, Sr.

Vengeance is mine; I will repay, saith the Lord.

Romans, 12:19

*Confront them with annihilation, and they will then survive;
plunge them in a deadly situation, and they will then live.
When people fall into danger; they are then able to strive for
victory.*

Sun Tzu, *The Art of War*

1

*Be extremely subtle, even to the point of formlessness. Be
extremely mysterious, even to the point of soundlessness.
Thereby you can be the director of the opponent's fate.*

Sun Tzu, *The Art of War*

Shortly after they landed on Laskar, the four men went out and
bought a car.

They paid cash for it, so Friendly Burl, the friendliest vehic
dealer in Laskar, was not fussy about such details as *Who are
you really?* and *Where have you come from?* Besides, he thought
he already knew the answer. Four gray and faceless suits;
probably on an illicit holiday; an escape from boss, sig-others,
kids.

'You guys planning on being in Laskar long?' asked Friendly
Burl of Burl's Friendly Vehics.

Two of the men carried briefcases; none of them carried
luggage.

'No,' said one of the suits, handing over the requisite number
of golden eagles.

The manner and tone in which the man said that single word
sucked the 'friendly' out of Burl and caused him to revise his
original estimate. These were not stressed-out execs. He began
immediately and somewhat nervously to count his money. Finding it correct, he relaxed.

'Salesmen, huh?' Burl ventured. He winked knowingly. 'Or
maybe not selling but dealing?'

The men did not answer. They put their briefcases in the car.

Buying a vehic rather than renting one on Laskar was not
unusual. Like everything and everyone else in the sin-soaked city
of Laskar, rental cars tended to lead brief, albeit exciting lives.

Consequently, rental dealers demanded a hefty amount of plastic up front. Insurance, they called it.

It cost a bit more to buy a vehic on Laskar, but the purchaser was generally glad to pay extra for the convenience and the peace of mind. Upon leaving the city, the car could always be resold – for scrap metal, if nothing else.

And paying in cash left no trail.

By now, Burl was really curious. He had a lot of friends and some of them in the city would be very interested in knowing if competition was about to move in.

'You fellers ever been to Laskar before?' Burl asked, eyeing the briefcases.

'No,' replied the same suit who had paid for the car. He was staring in the direction of the city, squinting against Laskar's garish green sun.

'Then you sure don't wanna lose your way drivin' around town,' Burl offered casually. 'If you'll tell me where you're going, I can give you directions.'

He waited hopefully. No response.

He tried again. 'I got a compu-map I can install in half-a-jiffy. No trouble. Just tell me where you're headed and I'll program it –'

'No,' said the suit.

The four men climbed into the car – an ordinary, midsize hover, nothing special, nothing fancy – and drove it off the lot. Two rode in the front, two in the back. Friendly Burl saw them off the lot, gave them a friendly wave, then hurried inside to contact a few 'friends.'

Friendly Burl's was conveniently located near the public spaceport, on the outskirts of the city. Finding the way to the city was easy – the only highway ran past the spaceport.

One man drove. The man seated in the front next to the driver navigated. The two in the back removed needle-guns from their inside suit jacket pockets, kept watch out the windows.

'All going according to plan, Knight Commander.' The hover's driver spoke into a small handheld voice-recorder.

The hover reached the entrance to the highway. Here a decision was required. Turn to the left and there, silhouetted against the green sky, were the high-rise whorehouses, the glitzy casinos, the holodomes of planet Laskar's major claim to fame, the city Laskar. Turn to the right and there were cactus and weird rock formations and eventually, a long distance away, the box-shaped barracks, the half-moon hangars, the sand-blasted tarmac of the Royal Naval Base.

Glancing up and down the highway, the driver said, 'How far is Snaga Ohme's from here?'

'Straight across country. About fifty kilometers,' was the reply.

Those fifty kilometers brought one to the palatial mansion and vast estate of the late Snaga Ohme, former weapons purveyor to the galaxy's rich and warlike. Several years previous, the wealthy Adonian had died, leaving his extensive and complicated financial affairs in complete disorder. To give him credit, Ohme had not expected to be murdered.

Always pleased to be able to help one of its citizens, the military had assisted Ohme's creditors by immediately seizing control of the Adonian's estate, including all weapons, designs for weapons, and prototypes of new weapons that the late Snaga Ohme had invented.

'Is Knight Officer Fuqua still inside the Ohme estate?'

'Yes, sir. But according to his latest report, his unit is due to transfer out anytime now. He'll have to leave with the unit, of course.'

The driver nodded. 'He has served his purpose. I doubt if we could learn anything more from him. We will proceed to Laskar.'

Arriving at the intersection, the hovercar turned left.

Laskar was not a planned community. Its streets had not been laid out according to any grand design. Rather, its buildings had sprung up like fungus, sprouting wherever the spores happened to fall. Buildings rarely faced each other, or fronted a street, but stood sideways to one another, like two hookers working the same block, who pretend to ignore each other yet keep a watchful eye on the competition. Consequently, the streets had been laid out around the buildings, which resulted in a great many serpentine roads, innumerable alleys, dead ends (aptly named), cul-de-sacs, and streets that had started out going somewhere only to end up lost and confused in the center of a very bad nowhere.

The four men were driving to one of the worst nowheres in Laskar.

Which was why there were four of them. And the needle-guns.

The navigator guided them unerringly through the maze of gambling dens, liquor bars, drug-bars, cyber-bars, blood-bars. They drove past the live sex, semi-live sex, semiconscious sex joints. They ignored the hookers of every age, race, sex, gender, and planetary origin. They paid scant attention to the occasional cop-shop – fortified bunkers from which the cops rarely emerged and then only to collect protection money that provided the citizens of Laskar protection against nobody but the cops.

'Travel down Painted Eye half a kilometer, sir. Turn north onto Snake Road. Brownstone walk-up. Number 757. Our man is on the top floor. Apartment 9e.'

No unnecessary talk between them. No names. The two men in the back were deferential to the two in the front, especially the driver. The two in back never spoke unless spoken to and then answered respectfully in as concise a manner as possible.

The driver, who was the leader, followed instructions, swerving sharply to avoid hitting a woman with an Adam's apple and a low-cut dress, revealing a hairy chest, who swore at them in a gravelly voice and gave the car a few savage kicks with her high heels as the hover skimmed past.

The driver pulled up in front of 757. He, the man in front, and one of the men in back got out of the car. The leader carried a briefcase. The second man had his hands free. The third man thrust his needle-gun into his suit coat pocket. The fourth man remained seated in the car. His needle-gun had been replaced by a beam rifle assembled from his briefcase. The rifle lay across his knees.

The leader stood on the cracked and litter-strewn sidewalk, gazing intently at the building, studying it carefully. It was nine stories high, made of brick formed from the local stone, which meant that it was sandy-colored and, in the heat of the late afternoon, took on a slightly greenish cast from Laskar's oddly colored sun. (The sun was not green. According to scientists, something in the atmosphere was, which gave the sun its strained-pea tinge. The natives were proud of their green sun, however, and disputed the scientific claim.)

Whether the green was in the sun or the sky, the sickly tint did nothing to improve the building's appearance, but rather gave it an unwholesome look. All the windows on the lower floor were boarded up, with graffiti scrawled across them. Here and there, on upper floors, TO RENT signs had been plastered onto cracked glass – the spots of white looked like an outbreak of the pox.

People on the sidewalk brushed past the men without a glance. The citizens of Laskar had their own problems to pursue, the tourists had their own pleasures, and none of them gave a damn about anyone else. A couple of bored-looking women in see-through plastic skirts sidled over to the driver and, in a few well-chosen words, described a possible evening's entertainment. The leader didn't even bother to answer and, with a shrug, the women sauntered off.

Several of the locals, lounging on the pavement, grinned and laughed, eyed the car with the expert air of those who know the current market value for that particular model, stripped down.

The leader paid no attention to them, either.

'Cover the back exit,' he ordered the man with the needle-gun.

'Yes, sir.'

The man with the needle-gun took off down a dark and grim-looking alleyway that smelled of body waste and garbage. A hand reached out – palm up – from a bundle of rags and cardboard as the man passed. A voice mumbled something unintelligible.

The man with the gun kept walking.

The beggar threw an empty jump-juice bottle at him. The bottle smashed into the pavement at the man's feet. He crunched calmly over the broken glass, continued into the noisome dark of the alleyway. He might have been less comfortable in his dangerous surroundings had he not been wearing full body armor beneath his nondescript suit.

The two men in front gave the third time to get into position. When a barely heard beep on a commlink informed them that he was ready, the two men mounted splintered and broken stairs – unquestionably the most dangerous obstacle they'd faced yet. Shoving open a rickety door, they walked inside the vestibule.

The leader took another careful look around.

'Security cam?'

11

'Temporarily out of order, sir,' was the answer.

The leader examined the entry door.

'It's locked, sir. Modern system. The owner doesn't want any homesteaders. We could blow it . . .'

The leader shook his head. He shifted the briefcase to his left hand, reached up, pressed the buzzer for 9e.

No response.

He pressed it again, this time held it longer.

No response.

He glanced at his subordinate.

'Bosk's inside, sir. He never leaves until after dark. But he'll be reluctant to answer the door. He's in debt. Local money-lender.'

The leader raised an eyebrow. He pressed the button again, spoke into the intercom. 'Bosk. You don't know me. I'm here on business. It could be worth your while to let me inside. I've got an offer to make you.'

Still no response.

The leader hit the button again. Leaning down to the intercom, he spoke two words clearly and distinctly. 'Negative waves.'

He stepped back, waited for as long as it might take a man to get up out of a chair, cross a small room.

There came a click on the lock of the entry door.

The leader and his subordinate entered, shut the door behind them. The leader again took a careful look around.

'You wait down here,' he said.

His subordinate took up a position in a shadowy corner beneath the staircase. From here, he could see, but not be readily seen. Outside, the locals approached the car, backed off hurriedly when they saw the beam rifle.

Folding his arms across his chest, the subordinate settled himself to wait.

The leader began to climb nine flights of stairs.

12

2

Vengeance, deep-brooding o'er the slain . . .
Sir Walter Scott, *The Lay of the Last Minstrel*

Bosk stood unsteadily by the door, staring at the intercom as if it could answer his questions. He was a little drunk. Bosk was always a little drunk these days. It eased his pain, cut the fear. He was always a little afraid these days, as well.

The intercom had no answers for him. The room seemed to heave a bit, and so Bosk – knowing that it would be a long wait while his guest climbed nine flights of stairs – stumbled back over and plunked himself down in his dilapidated recliner.

Directly across the room from him, the vid was blaring loudly. James M. Warden, personable television personality, was conducting an interview with His Royal Majesty, Dion Starfire.

Bosk gulped a swig of jump-juice from a cracked glass, focused blearily on the screen.

The young king was answering a question about the late Warlord Derek Sagan.

'He was not perfect. No man is perfect,' His Majesty was saying gravely. 'He made mistakes.'

'I beg your pardon, Your Majesty,' James M. Warden respectfully contradicted, 'but some might consider the word *mistakes* inappropriate for what many consider to be heinous crimes.'

'Try *murder!*' Bosk yelled loudly at the screen.

His Majesty was shaking his head, almost as if he'd heard Bosk's comment. 'Lord Sagan was a warrior. He acted out of his own warrior code, which, as you know, is a harsh one. But he held to that code with honor. He took part in the revolution because he believed that the government under my late uncle's rule was corrupt and ineffective. That it was about to collapse into anarchy, which would have put all the people in the galaxy in the gravest danger.

'When Lord Sagan discovered that the new government under

13

President Peter Robes was every bit as corrupt as the old, the Warlord concluded that he – one of the few surviving members of the Blood Royal – had the right to try to seize control. Circumstances, the Creator, Fate – call it what you will – intervened. Lord Sagan's ambitious and, some might say, his despotic plans failed.'

King Starfire's hand clenched. The famous Starfire blue eyes were lit from within by a radiance that looked well on the vidscreens. The red-golden lion's mane of hair framed a face that was youthful, handsome, earnest, intense. His godlike looks, his vibrant personality – all were rapidly making a reluctant deity of a very mortal young man.

'But I tell you, Mr Warden, and I tell my people that I would not be here now, I would not be wearing this crown, the galaxy would not be at peace today, if it were not for the sacrifices of Lord Derek Sagan. He attempted to correct the great wrongs he had done and, in so doing, gave his life that others might live. He is one of the greatest men I have ever known. I will always honor his memory.'

Bosk tossed the remainder of the jump-juice at the vidscreen. 'Here's that for his fuckin' memory.' The juice trickled down the screen, soaked into the threadbare carpet which covered the floor of the shabby studio apartment.

A crisp knock sounded on the door.

Lurching to his feet, Bosk went to answer it. On his way, he made a detour to the bottle, poured himself another drink. Reaching the door, he peeped out the one-way peephole, saw a man dressed in a suit, carrying a briefcase. The man didn't look threatening. He didn't look anything. He had one of those faces you meet and five minutes later you can't recall ever having been introduced to him before. Bosk was more interested in the briefcase. It is said that Adonians can smell money.

Bosk's nose twitched. He opened the door.

'Yeah?' he said, looking first at the briefcase, then finally lifting his gaze to meet the stranger's. 'What's the deal?'

'I don't believe it would be wise for us to conduct our business in the hallway,' the stranger said. He wasn't even breathing hard after the long climb. He smiled in a pleasant and disarming

14

manner. 'Your neighbors don't need to know your affairs, do they?'

Bosk followed the stranger's glance, saw Mrs Kasper standing in her half-open door. He glared at her.

'I heard a knock,' she said defensively. 'Thought it might be for me.' She sniffed. 'Another of your "clients"?'

'Nosy old bitch!' Bosk retorted. He opened his own door wider. 'C'mon in, then.'

The stranger entered. Bosk shut the door, took a look out the peephole to make sure Mrs Kasper had gone back into her apartment. She had a bad habit of loitering in the hall, listening outside closed doors.

Sure enough.

Bosk flung the door open, nearly knocking Mrs Kasper down.

'Care to join us?' He leered.

Disgusted, she flounced back inside her apartment and slammed her door.

Bosk shut his door again, turned around to face his guest. The stranger was tall, well-built, handsome if you went for older guys with hair graying at the temples, which Bosk did not. The clothes were expensive but not ostentatious. Snaga Ohme would have approved the choice of colors: muted blues and grays. The face was a mask. The lines and wrinkles had been trained to betray nothing of the thoughts within. The eyes were one-way mirrors. Bosk looked in, saw himself reflected back.

Having once been close to some of the most powerful people in the galaxy, Bosk recognized and appreciated the quiet air of control and authority this man exuded, like a fine cologne that never overwhelms, never cloys the senses.

'I assume that you are the Adonian known as Bosk?' The stranger was polite.

'I'm an Adonian and my name's Bosk. That answer your questions?'

'Not all of them.' The stranger continued to be polite. 'Were you once in the employ of the late Snaga Ohme, former weapons dealer?'

Bosk swallowed. 'I wasn't in his "employ," mister! I was his goddamn friend! His best friend. He trusted me, more'n anyone. He trusted me. I knew . . . all his secrets.'

Bosk brushed his hand across his eyes, wiped his nose with his fingers. Adonians are a sensitive race, who have a tendency to get maudlin when they're drunk. 'I was his confidant. Me. Not those other fops, those pretty boys – fawning and preening. And the women. They were the worst. But he loved me. He loved me.'

Bosk drained the glassful of jump-juice.

The stranger nodded. 'Yes, that is consistent with my information. Snaga Ohme told you all his secrets. He even told you about his project code-named Negative Waves.'

'Maybe, maybe not.' Bosk eyed the stranger warily. 'You want a drink?'

'No, thank you. Mind if I sit down?'

'Suit yourself.' Bosk wandered back to the bottle.

The stranger walked across the small room. Bosk watched him out of the corner of his eye. The stranger's movements were fluid, controlled. He was in excellent physical condition, with a hard-muscled body, good reflexes.

Pity he's not twenty years younger, Bosk thought.

The stranger pulled up a battered metal fold-out chair – one of the few articles of furniture in the apartment. In front of the chair was a computer. A highly sophisticated and expensive personal computer, it looked considerably out of place in the poverty-stricken surroundings. The stranger seated himself in the chair, regarded the computer with admiration.

'That's a fine setup, Bosk. Probably worth the price of this whole apartment building.'

'I'd sell myself first,' Bosk said sullenly. He *had* sold himself first, but that was beside the point. He hunched back down in the recliner. 'Snaga Ohme gave that computer to me. It's one of the best, the fastest in the whole damn galaxy.'

A photograph of Snaga Ohme – bronze, beautiful, as were most Adonians – stood in an honored place beside the crystalline storage lattice.

The stranger nodded, smiled in sympathy, placed the briefcase on his knees, and waited for Bosk to resume talking. But Bosk's attention had been recaptured by the vidscreen. The king was speaking again, this time about the long-expected and widely anticipated birth of the royal heir.

'Fuckin' bastard,' muttered Bosk. 'I hate the fuckin' bastard.

16

Him and that fuckin' Derek Sagan. Wasn't for that fuckin' Derek Sagan, *he'd* be alive today.'

A glance at the photograph of Snaga Ohme clarified the pronoun.

'Tell me about Derek Sagan, Bosk,' the stranger suggested.

Bosk tore his gaze from the vid. 'Why d'you wanna know about Derek Sagan?'

'Because he was the reason for the Negative Waves project, wasn't he, Bosk?'

Bosk hesitated, regarded the stranger suspiciously. But the Adonian had had far too much to drink to make the mental effort to play games, keep secrets. Besides, what did it matter anyway? Ohme was dead. And when his life had ended, so had Bosk's. He didn't even have revenge to keep him going anymore. So he nodded.

'Yeah. Sagan was. I don't care who knows it. If His Majesty sent you – '

'His Majesty didn't send me, Bosk.' The stranger leaned back comfortably in the chair. 'His Majesty doesn't give a damn about you, and you know it. Nobody gives a damn, do they, Bosk?'

'You do, apparently,' Bosk said with a cunning not even the jump-juice could completely drown.

'I do, Bosk.' The stranger opened the briefcase. 'I care a lot.'

Bosk stared. The briefcase was filled with plastic chips – black plastic chips, stamped in gold, arranged in neat stacks.

Bosk rose slowly to his feet to get a better look, half afraid that the liquor might be playing tricks on his mind. It had been almost four years since the night Snaga Ohme had been murdered. Four years since the night Warlord Derek Sagan had seized control of the dead man's mansion and its wealth. That night, as Sagan's army marched in the front, Bosk had exited the mansion via the secret tunnels in the back.

During these intervening four years, Bosk had never seen *one* black chip stamped in gold, much less . . . how many were in that briefcase? . . . He took a conservative guess on the number of chips in each stack, counted the number of stacks across, counted the number of stacks down, did some muddled multiplication, and drew in a shivering breath.

17

'Twenty thousand, Bosk,' said the stranger. 'It's all yours. Today.'

Bosk found his chair with the backs of his legs, sat down rather suddenly. Life up till now had been an endless lineup of jump-juice bottles, selling his favors in cheap bars and bathhouses, and dodging the local collection agency.

'I could go back to Adonia,' he said, staring at the black chips.

'You could leave tonight, Bosk,' said the stranger.

Bosk licked dry lips, took another drink, gulped it the wrong way, coughed. 'What do you want?'

'You know,' said the stranger. 'You tried to sell it a couple of years ago. Bad timing. No market.'

'Negative Waves.' Bosk's gaze strayed to the computer.

The stranger nodded, closed the lid of the briefcase. The light seemed to go out of the room.

'Tell me about the project, Bosk. Tell me everything you can remember.'

'Why do you want to know?'

'Just to make sure we're talking about the same project.'

A mental hand was tugging at the coattails of Bosk's brain, trying to get his attention. But the jump-juice and the gold-stamped black chips combined to cause him to shoo it away.

'Yeah, sure,' Bosk said. He reached for his glass, discovered it was empty, started to head for the bottle.

He found the stranger holding on to it. Bosk staggered back, blinked. He had no clear recollection of seeing the stranger move, yet the man was standing right in front of him.

'We'll have a drink to celebrate closing the deal,' said the stranger, smiling and holding on to the bottle. 'Not before.' He walked back to his seat by the computer.

Bosk was going to get angry and then decided he wasn't. Shrugging, he went back to his chair. The stranger returned to the folding chair, set the bottle down next to the computer, beside the picture of Snaga Ohme. On his way past, the stranger flicked off the vid. Congenial reporter James M. Warden and His Majesty the King dwindled to insignificant dots, then were gone.

A commentary on life, Bosk thought, staring at the empty screen with watery eyes.

'Where should I begin?'

'The space-rotation bomb,' specified the stranger.

Bosk glared, suspicions returned. 'You *must* be from the king. No one else knew about that.'

'I'm not from the king, Bosk,' the stranger said patiently. 'Maybe someday I'll tell you where I *am* from. But for now, I'd say you're being paid enough not to be curious. Let me help things along. *We* know about the space-rotation bomb. We know how Warlord Sagan came up with the design for it. How he needed someone to build it. Needed it done quick and quiet, because he was planning to overthrow the galactic government. And so he went to Snaga Ohme.'

'The only man in the universe who could have built that damn bomb,' Bosk said with moist-eyed pride. He sniffed, wiped his nose with the back of his hand. 'Whoever had that bomb coulda overthrown six billion governments.' He gazed back into the past, shook his head in admiration. 'It was sweet. Best work Ohme ever did. He said so himself. Blow a hole in the fabric of the universe. Destroy all life as we know it.'

'That was only theorized.'

Bosk waved his hand, irritated at the stranger's slowness of thought. 'That's not the point. Blackmail. The threat. Hold it over their heads. Sword of something-er-other – '

'Damocles,' said the stranger.

Bosk shrugged, not interested. He coughed, licked his lips, looked longingly at the bottle.

The stranger ignored the look. 'Ohme built the bomb according to the Warlord's specifications, using Sagan's financing. But then it occurred to Ohme that, with this bomb in the Warlord's possession, Derek Sagan might get a – shall we say – swelled head?'

'Snaga Ohme was the most powerful man in the galaxy,' Bosk averred. 'The top weapons dealer and manufacturer alive. No one could touch him. Kings, warlords, governors, congressmen, corporate leaders – they all came running when he so much as twitched his pinkie their direction.'

'Ohme feared that the Warlord – if and when he came to power – might put him out of business. So Ohme built the negative wave device to kill Derek Sagan.'

Bosk shook his head vehemently. 'Not kill him.'

'Keep Sagan in line, then.'

'If he leaned on us, we could lean back.' Bosk was defensive. 'We were looking out for our own interests.'

'Sagan has the bomb, blackmails the government. Ohme has the negative wave device, blackmails Sagan.'

'It was an ingenious idea. You gotta admit that.'

'All predicated on the fact that Sagan was specially genetically designed. One of the Blood Royal. The device would kill him and him alone, even in a crowd. Yes, a truly remarkable concept. *If* it worked . . .'

Bosk snorted. 'It worked, all right.'

'Ohme tested it?' The stranger appeared surprised, intrigued. 'We weren't aware that he'd built a working model.'

Bosk opened his mouth, suddenly closed it again. He shrugged, surly now, and deciding to be uncooperative. Who was this bastard? Coming here with all his damn stupid questions. And how the hell did he know so much? What was going on?

Standing up, a bit unsteadily, Bosk stalked over, grabbed the bottle, stalked back, and poured himself a drink. He flopped down in the chair, reached for the remote, turned on the vid. James M. Warden was resurrected. He was still interviewing His Majesty the King. Her Majesty the Queen had joined them.

The mental hand that had been tugging at Bosk's brain gave him a sudden sharp jab that made him flinch, literally. He saw it all now. Everything became suddenly clear, as clear as it could be through a liquor-soaked haze.

You juice-head, he swore at himself. You damn near let him walk off with this for a measly twenty thou. It's worth ten times – hell, make that a hundred times – more!

Bosk stared hard at the vidscreen, his brain flopping around, wondering how best to appear completely unconscious of the fact that he'd scammed the whole scheme and that it was big, really big, and that he was going to make a bloody fortune off it.

I can't let on that I know, though, was his next thought, which of course made him wonder if he'd already given himself away. He slid a glance over to the stranger, slid it back quickly. The stranger was staring at the screen, too, but with the abstracted gaze of one who is using a visual aid to enhance far-removed thoughts.

20

Bosk breathed easier. Noticing his hand was clenched around the glass so tightly that his knuckles had turned white, he forced himself to relax. He started to take a drink, then thought better of it, then was afraid that not taking a drink might seem suspicious. He brought the glass to his lips, set it down again untasted, and wondered uneasily how to bring the conversation around to where he wanted it.

At that moment, James M. Warden broke for a message from his sponsor.

Bosk cleared his throat. 'What I meant to say is that the theory behind the device was sound. Ohme knew it would work. There was no reason to doubt it. It's all in there.' Bosk gazed fondly at the computer.

'You ended up with the design,' said the stranger.

'I ended up with it,' Bosk said softly. 'It was my chance, you see. My chance to get even. The night Ohme was murdered, all hell broke loose. Sagan's troops had the goddamn place surrounded. In the confusion, I raided Ohme's own personal computer. I downloaded, then destroyed, all the files on the Negative Waves project. I'm the *only* person alive who's got them.'

Bosk added the last with emphasis. He was watching the vidscreen with a smile on his face, felt emboldened enough to repeat himself. 'I'm the only one.'

The stranger nodded. 'Yes, so I understand. You searched for backers to finance the project. But with the government collapsed and the new king taking over, no one was interested in spending a fortune on a weapon with such limited potential.'

'Sagan was still alive,' Bosk muttered.

'True, Warlord Sagan was still alive and had enemies. But by the time they might have been willing to invest, Derek Sagan had managed to get himself killed. He was the last of the Blood Royal – the only people Ohme's device was designed to destroy. The demand for your product went right down the toilet.'

'Not the *last* of the Blood Royal,' Bosk said, with a sly glance at the vidscreen. 'Sagan wasn't the last. The king. Dion Starfire. *He's* the last.'

The stranger was nonplussed. 'There could be others.'

'Sure, sure.' Bosk staggered to his feet. His unsteady hand knocked his glass to the floor. 'What do you take me for? A brain-rotted old queen, too juiced to know who I'm climbing in bed with? This is big. Really big. Bigger than twenty thousand fuckin' eagles. I'll go back to Adonia. I'll go back in style. No more hanging around the Laskar bars, letting guys like you in your expensive suits think you're doin' me some big honor by rubbing your ass against mine, then throwin' me out the next morning like I was too filthy to live. You need me, damn it. You need me and I want my share or I'll . . . I'll . . .'

'You'll what, Bosk?' asked the stranger calmly.

Bosk realized too late that he'd gone too far. Fear knotted his belly, sent the gastric juices surging up, bile-bitter and burning, into his throat. His jaws ached; saliva flooded his mouth. He was afraid he might vomit.

He swallowed several times. Sweat, cold and clammy, chilled on his body, made him shiver.

'I'll find other buyers.' He decided to bluff it out.

The stranger considered, said gravely, 'Very well, Bosk. We'll meet your price. Just think of this as a down payment.' He patted the briefcase.

Bosk didn't like it. The guy had given in far too quickly. Still, the Adonian reflected, I *have* got him by the short hairs.

'You'll need a technical adviser.' Bosk slurred his words. The shivering fear caused a tremor in his right leg. He clamped his hand over his leg, to stop the muscle jerking. 'There's a lot of data . . . I left out . . . not in . . . the files.'

'Bound to be,' the stranger agreed. He stood up from the folding chair. Placing the briefcase on the table next to the picture of Snaga Ohme, the stranger smiled, indicated the computer screen. 'Bring up the files. I want to see what I'm buying.'

Bosk hesitated. 'It'll take a while to get the material all in order. Big files, scattered. I'm not all that organized.'

'I understand completely. I just want to take a look before I go. Scan it, get a feel for the project. That's all. I think that's only fair, considering my initial investment. Then, when you have the data compiled, I'll be back to pick it up. At that time, I'll bring the rest of your payment. Besides,' the stranger added with a slight lift of his shoulders, 'I'd like to know the project's really in that computer of yours.'

'It's in there,' Bosk said, gloating. 'And it'll work.' He stumbled over to the chair, sat down in front of the computer.

Bosk placed his hands on the input keypads. After a second's wait, the screen began to glow. A red light flashed; the log-on script for Bosk came up on the screen. He had yet to hit any keys. Once the sequence was complete, the menu appeared.

Bosk cast a cunning glance at the stranger. 'Why don't you go take a look at the view. Or maybe you should check to make sure no one's stolen your car.'

The stranger smiled to indicate he understood completely. Leaving the vicinity of the computer, he strode nonchalantly over to the window and peered out through the grime to the street below.

Once the stranger's back was turned, Bosk accessed a file titled 'Classical Literature through the Ages' – guaranteed to be a snorer. Opening that, he selected the choice: 'Idylls of the King.'

The computer responded by demanding a retina scan.

Bosk moved his face closer to the screen, flinched as the scanning beam swiftly crossed his eyeball ten thousand times.

The word 'verified' appeared on the screen, followed by a display that did not appear to be, on first glance, classical literature.

'All right,' Bosk said after several minutes had elapsed, silent minutes punctuated by the clicking sounds of the Adonian's fingers on the keyboard and muted voice commands to the computer's audio interpreter.

He gestured at the screen. 'There it is. Negative Waves. I've brought up the outline of the initial concept, plus the preliminary diagrams of what the weapon should look like when it's completed. I figure that should be enough to convince you that what I've got is the real thing.'

The stranger left the window. Hands clasped behind his back, he strode over to the computer. He bent down to see the screen, leaning over Bosk, who had remained seated. The stranger studied the text intently.

'Scroll on further,' he said, making no move to touch the keyboard.

Bosk obediently, and proudly, did so. He, too, was reading the text, written in Snaga Ohme's precise, organized, meticulous style. The concept was sound. It would work. Bosk raised his hand, reverently touched the computer screen.

'Genius,' he murmured.

'Indeed,' said the stranger, and he sounded impressed.

Bosk heard the stranger straighten. The Adonian turned around, grinning in elation, prepared to name what he considered his absolute minimum price for the files and his knowledge concerning them, and found a handheld lasgun within ten centimeters of the bridge of his nose.

Terror surged. He opened his mouth to beg . . . scream . . .

With careful precision, the stranger shot Bosk through the center of the forehead. The beam bored a neat bloodless hole through bone and brain. The Adonian slumped, slid out of the chair.

The stranger shoved the body aside, sat down in the chair. 'Damn,' he muttered softly.

Without Bosk's hands on the keyboard, the screen had gone blank.

The stranger was only momentarily thwarted, however. Though he had not anticipated this problem, he was prepared to deal with it. He spoke calmly into his commlink. 'It's finished. Come up.'

Bending over the corpse, the stranger slid what appeared to be plastic thimbles over Bosk's fingertips. Then, adjusting his lasgun's intensity, the stranger modified the beam to a cutting tool and proceeded to remove Bosk's right eyeball. This grisly task completed, he placed the freshly severed eyeball in a holder, stood the holder on the table next to the computer. He then removed the fingertip plastics, now bearing the whorls and lines of Bosk's fingerprints. Carefully, the stranger drew them over his own fingers.

Seating himself at the computer, he rested his fingers on the keypad of the blanked computer.

The screen logged in 'Bosk.' The menu appeared.

Studying the list, the stranger hesitated. There was, no doubt, a trap in here. Even if he happened to guess the right file, bringing it up in the wrong sequence might cause it to self-destruct.

Unable to discover even a hint of a clue, the stranger exited the

24

menu. Bosk had been smart, but he had also been lazy. Hopefully too lazy to make certain all the doors into his files had been shut and locked.

Hands on the keyboard, the stranger typed – in case the computer was attuned to Bosk's voice – the command: 'Recall last accessed project.' An old trick, but it worked.

A file appeared. Words, arranged in a definite pattern, filled the screen; words in a language long dead and forgotten by all but a few. The stranger was among the few who could read them, but this wasn't what he was after. He tensed. The computer scrolled down to the lines:

> Wearing the white flower of a blameless life,
> Before a thousand peering littlenesses,
> In that fierce light which beats upon a throne,
> And blackens every blot.

Suddenly, 'Idylls of the King' disappeared. The screen went blank. This was either what he was searching for or he'd lost it.

The stranger picked up the eyeball, held it to the retina scan. A file came up. He read the header and smiled.

'Negative Waves.'

3

You're not a man, you're a machine.
George Bernard Shaw, *Arms and the Man*

The Wiedermann Detective Agency, with offices in every major city of every major planet in the heart of the galaxy, handled only cases that were far too important, discreet, and delicate for other, less sophisticated (and less expensive) agencies. The Wiedermann Agency would not, for example, tail your philandering husband unless he happened to be the prime minister and the ensuing scandal could topple a government.

The agency was expert in corporate intrigue, both detecting it and performing it. They did not handle ordinary or sordid cases.

They would negotiate with terrorists and kidnappers for you, but it would cost you plenty. They would not undertake to break your uncle out of prison, or remove him from a penal colony, but they would refer you to people who did that sort of thing. They would not find out who poisoned your sister unless you had proof that the local police were being deliberately obtuse and your credit rating indicated you could pay for a prolonged investigation.

The agency's offices were always located in upscale downtown professional buildings, rubbing shoulders comfortably with law firms that had twenty-seven names on the letterhead, and the offices of doctors whose names were followed by that many initials. The agency's own offices were spacious, elegantly appointed, a soothing gray-blue in color scheme. Corporate head-quarters were located on Inner Rankin, the smaller and more exclusive planet of a two-planet system, the larger planet (indus-trial base) being known as Outer Rankin.

Only the most important clients were ever permitted to enter the agency's corporate headquarters, which was why the recep-tionist – a live, human receptionist – placed her finger on the security button when the cyborg walked through the main doors.

It was a long walk from the main doors – steelglass, blastproof – across the polished floor to the receptionist's desk, and so she had time to get a good look at the cyborg. He had obviously made a mistake.

The Wiedermann Agency took on cyborgs as clients, but such cyborgs were sophisticated types. Expensive body jobs. Not even their own mothers could have guessed they were more metal than flesh. Plastiskin and flesh-foam, muscle-gel and quiet-as-a-whisper motors, battery packs and pumps enabled most cyborgs to blend in with ordinary flesh-and-blood beings, the main differ-ence being that cyborgs always tended to look just a bit *too* perfect – as if they'd been tailor-made, not picked up off the rack.

This particular cyborg was, however, what the receptionist would classify (did classify, for security purposes) as 'hard labor.' Most planets sent their convicted felons to hard-labor camps. Located on frontier planets or moons, these camps were generally mining communities or agricultural collectives. The work was hard, physical, and often dangerous. Those prisoners injured in accidents were provided cybernetic limbs and other body parts made to be strong, efficient, and cheap – not cosmetic.

This cyborg was bald. Acid burn scars mottled the skin on his head. His eyes – one of which was real, both of which were dark and brooding – were set deep beneath an overhanging forehead. His right hand was flesh, his left hand metal.

The security diagnostic that came up on the receptionist's recessed screen disclosed that seventy percent of the cyborg's body was artificial: left side, hand, leg, foot, face, skull, ear, eye. But the receptionist could see this for herself. Unlike any other cyborg she had encountered, this one scorned to hide his replacement parts. In fact, he appeared to flaunt them.

He wore combat fatigues that had been cut off at the hip on the left leg, revealing a broad expanse of gleaming, compartmented, and jointed metal. The left sleeve of his shirt was rolled up over the metal arm, revealing a series of LED lights that flickered occasionally, performing periodic systems checks. His metal hand could apparently be detached from the wrist, to judge by the locking mechanism, and replaced with different hands – or tools.

His age was indeterminate, scar tissue having replaced most of the original flesh of his face. But the right half of his body – the half that was still human – was in excellent physical condition. Arm muscles bulged; chest and thigh muscles were smooth, well defined. He walked with a peculiar gait, as if the two halves of his body weren't quite in sync with one another.

Truly, he was one of the worst cyber-jobs the receptionist had ever seen.

'I would have sued,' she muttered to herself, and put on the Wiedermann smile, which would be completely wasted on this man, who had probably come in to use the toilet.

'Good morning, sir,' said the receptionist, giving the cyborg the smile but not the Wiedermann warmth that was reserved for paying clients. 'How can I help you?' She could hear, as the cyborg approached the desk, the faint hum of his machinery.

'The name's Xris,' he said, a mechanical tinge to his voice. 'I received a subspace transmission. Told to be here, this building, eleven hundred hours.' He glanced around without curiosity, but appeared to note in one swift overview every object in the large

27

room, including – from a momentary pause and stare – the surveillance devices.

The receptionist was confused for a moment, then remembered.

'You're applying for the janitor's job. I'm afraid you've made a mistake. They should have told you to use the rear entrance –'

'Sister.' The cyborg placed his flesh hand and his metal hand on either side of her, leaned over her. She was disconcerted to see the artificial eye readjust its focus as his head drew nearer. 'I told you. I have an appointment.'

'I'll check the files,' she said coldly.

'You do that, sister.'

'What was the name?'

'Xris. With an X. Pronounced "Chris," in case you're interested.'

She wasn't. 'Surname.'

'Xris'll do. There's only one of me.'

The receptionist flashed him a look which said the universe could undoubtedly count this as a blessing, then brought up the appointment calendar on a screen beneath the gleaming glass top of her desk. Her fingers flicked over the smooth surface.

The cyborg glanced around the reception area again, noted a security-bot glide out of a recess in the wall. Casually, Xris reached into the pocket of his shirt, drew out a golden and silver cigarette case, adorned with a shield on the top. The receptionist, had she been looking, would have been highly impressed. The shield was the crest of the Starfire family, belonged to the young king. The case was, in fact, a gift from the king. Xris opened the lid and withdrew an ugly, braided, foul-smelling form of tobacco known as a twist. He thrust the twist in his mouth, started to light it with the thumb of the metal hand.

'No smoking.' The receptionist indicated a sign to that effect.

Xris shrugged, doused the light. Keeping the twist in his mouth, he began to chew on it. 'Got any place I can spit?'

The receptionist glanced up, eyes narrowed in disgust, but she had located his name on the calendar and was therefore obligated to add the Wiedermann warmth to the Wiedermann smile, which had, unfortunately, slipped slightly.

'I'm sorry for the confusion, Mr … Xris. You are to see Mr Wiedermann.'

28

Xris continued to chew reflectively. 'Wiedermann himself, huh? I'm impressed.'

'That is Mr Wiedermann the younger,' clarified the receptionist, as if, yes, Xris should be impressed but only moderately. '*Not* Mr Wiedermann the elder. Please proceed to the eighteenth floor. Someone will meet you there, escort you to Mr Wiedermann's office. Put this badge on your pocket. Wear it at all times. Please do not take it off. This would activate our alarm system.'

Xris accepted the badge, clipped it on the pocket of his fatigues. 'About that janitor's job . . .' he began conversationally.

'I'm sorry for the mistake,' the receptionist said coldly. The Wiedermann smile could have, by now, been packaged and frozen. 'Please go on up. Mr Wiedermann doesn't like to be kept waiting.'

She answered a buzz from the commlink. She didn't like being around cyborgs, even the well-oiled.

The cyborg circled her desk to reach the lifts. The receptionist was talking to a prospective client. A touch of metal on her shoulder made her jump, flinch, so that she accidentally disconnected the call.

'I was about to say, you couldn't afford me,' Xris told her. 'Sister.'

Taking the twist out of his mouth, he tossed the soggy, half-chewed mass in the receptionist's trash disposer, then walked off.

It shouldn't gnaw at him, but it did. Gnawed at the part of him that hadn't been – couldn't be – replaced by machinery. People in general, women in particular – the way they looked at him. Or didn't look at him.

You asked for it, you know.

'Yeah, that's true,' Xris agreed with himself. Taking out another twist, he stuck it in his mouth, clamped down on it hard with his teeth.

But he preferred the pity, the disgust to be up front. Better that than later. Behind closed doors.

Not that there ever was a later. A door that ever closed.

It happens to all cyborgs, eventually. Even the 'pretty' ones. Sure, when she digs her nails into your fake flesh, it'll bleed fake blood – the miracle of modern technology. But when you hold her close, she'll hear the drone, the whine, the rhythmic clicks. And her flesh, her living flesh, grows cold in your arms, grows cold to your sensor devices. She realizes a machine's making love to her. She thinks: I might as well be screwing a toaster . . .

The lift had stopped. It had been stopped for some time, apparently, for it kept repeating 'Floor eighteen' in a manner that was beginning to sound irritated.

Berating himself – My God! How many years has it been since the operation anyway? Nine? Ten? – Xris strode off the lift. A young man, dressed in a tweed suit, tie, and knife-creased pants, was waiting for him.

'Xris? How do you do? I'm Dave Baldwin.' The young man extended a hand, didn't wince at Xris's grip, even gave as good as he got. 'Mr Wiedermann's expecting you.'

Turning, Baldwin led Xris down a carpeted hallway, done in muted tones, with muted lighting, polished woods, and the piped-in sounds of a string quartet. Occasionally, passing by an office with its door open, Xris glanced inside to see someone working at a computer or talking on a commlink. In one, he saw several people seated around a large polished wooden table holding cups of coffee and small electronic notepads.

'Where's your shoulder holster?' Xris asked.

The young man smiled faintly. 'I left mine in my other suit.'

'Sorry. I guess you must hear that all the time.'

'It's the detective vids,' Baldwin explained. 'People believe that stuff. When they see these offices and they find out that we look just as boring as any other office place, they're disappointed. We've had a few even walk out. Mr Wiedermann – that's the older Mr Wiedermann – once suggested that we should all dress the part. Wear guns. Smell like bourbon. Go around in our shirtsleeves with slouch hats on. We think he was kidding.'

'Was he?'

'You can never tell with old Mr Wiedermann,' Baldwin said carefully. 'I know our appearance disillusions people, especially when they find out that most of the trails we follow are paper. The only footprints we trace are electronic. We don't tail beautiful mysterious women in mink stoles. We do file-searches until we find some tiny little discrepancy in her personal finances which proves she's a spy or an embezzler or whatever. We study psychological profiles, sociological patterns.'

The young man stopped, eyed Xris quizzically. 'But you know all this, don't you, sir? I've read up on your case,' he added in explanation. 'You used to work for the investigative branch of the old democracy.'

'I was a Fed.' Xris nodded. 'But we wore holsters.'

Baldwin shook his head, obviously sympathetic. 'Mr Wiedermann's office is at the end of the corridor.'

'The younger,' Xris clarified.

'Right. The elder's almost fully retired now. Through this door.'

Through a door, into an outer office that appeared to be used as a storage room for boxes of computer paper, stacks of file folders, stacks of plastic disks, old-fashioned reels of magnetic tape, mags, actual bound books, all thrown together in no particular order.

'Mr Wiedermann doesn't like secretaries,' Baldwin explained in a low tone, pausing in front of the closed door of the inner office. 'He says he's seen too many ruin their bosses. The staff take turns running his errands for him. He's a genius.'

'He must be,' Xris observed, glancing at the clutter. 'Either that or Daddy owns the company.'

'He's a genius,' Baldwin said quietly. 'He doesn't often see clients. Your case interested him. I must say it was unique in *my* experience.'

He tapped on the door. 'Mr Wiedermann.' Opening it a crack, he peered inside. 'Mr Xris here – by appointment.'

'In!' came an irritable-sounding voice.

Baldwin opened the door wider, permitted Xris to enter. Giving the cyborg a reassuring smile, the young man asked if he could bring coffee, tea. Bourbon.

Xris shook his head.

'Good luck, sir. Have a seat. Say your name a couple of times, just to remind him you're here.'

Baldwin left, shutting the door behind him.

Xris looked at Mr Wiedermann, the younger.

A thin man with a pale face and a shock of uncombed sandy blond hair sat behind what might have been a desk. It was completely covered over, hidden by various assorted objects, some of which had apparently been elbowed out by others and were now lying on the floor.

Mr Wiedermann not acknowledging his presence, Xris glanced around the room. It had no windows, was lit by a single lamp on the desk, and by the lambent light shining from twenty separate computer screens that formed a semicircle behind the man's chair. The rest of the room was in shadow.

Wiedermann sat with his chin in his hands – his hands bent so that the chin rested on the backs, not the palms – perusing a document of some sort, studying it with rapt, single-minded intensity. He breathed through his mouth. A bow tie – clipped to the open collar – slanted off at an odd angle.

Xris removed a stack of files from a chair, kicked aside the clutter surrounding the desk, dragged the chair over, and placed it on the newly made bare spot on the floor.

Wiedermann never looked up.

Xris had just about figured this seeming abstraction was an affectation and was starting to grow irritated, when the blond-haired man lifted his gaze.

He stared at Xris with watery, very bright green eyes, said, 'I've been expecting you.'

The glow of the computer screens behind him cast an eerie halolike effect over the man. That and the darkened room made Xris think he'd accidentally broken in on some weird religious service.

Xris opened his mouth to introduce himself, but Wiedermann had shifted his attention to his desk. He made a sudden dive at a pile, snagged and pulled out – from about a quarter of the way down – a thick manila folder. The removal of the folder sent everything that had been stacked on top of it cascading to the floor. Xris leaned down to pick them up.

'Don't touch them,' Wiedermann snapped.

He opened the file folder, flipped through the contents quickly. Satisfied, he returned the green-eyed gaze to Xris.

'A gatherer,' Wiedermann said.

'I beg your pardon?' Xris blinked.

'I'm a gatherer. As in hunter/gatherer. Racial memory. Our ancestors. Men were hunters, women gatherers. Men went out, hunted food. Women foraged. Men could find game almost anywhere. Women had to remember where the berry patches were located from one year to the next, even after the tribe had moved from one hunting ground to another. Nature gave women the ability to remember the location of various objects that would guide them to the food.

'Take a woman. Show her unrelated objects scattered at random on a desk. Remove her from the room. Thirty minutes later, ask her what object was where and odds are she'll be able to remember. A man, given the same test, won't have a clue. I'm a gatherer, myself. I suppose, over the centuries, some of the gender lines have been obscured.'

It occurred to Xris that a lot more than Wiedermann's gender lines had been obscured, but the cyborg kept quiet. Wiedermann did not expect a response, apparently. He was no longer paying attention to his client, had begun flipping through the myriad documents in the file.

Xris shifted restlessly. Tiny beeps from his cybernetic arm and the faint hum of his battery pack blended with the hum of the various computers behind Wiedermann. The detective continued to peruse the file, but Xris had the impression that Wiedermann's thoughts had drifted off somewhere else.

Xris decided it was time those thoughts returned to him.

'Uh, look, Mr Wiedermann – '

'Ed. Ed Wiedermann. The younger.'

'Fine. You sent for me, Ed. I take it that means you've made some progress on my case?'

'Yes. Yes, we have.' Wiedermann nodded, continued to study the file. 'We've completed it successfully, in fact.'

The surge that went through Xris had nothing to do with his batteries. Elation sparked, its jolt nearly stopping his heart with bright, intense pleasure. He spent a moment reveling in the triumph, then said slowly, 'You mean you've found him. Rowan.'

'Dalin Rowan.' Wiedermann savored the name. 'We're close. Very close.'

Xris shut his eyes. Emotion brought tears, burned behind the lids. His hand – his good hand, resting on his good knee – clenched into a tight fist. Nails dug into his flesh. Good flesh, warm flesh. Blood – warm blood, real blood – throbbed in his temples. A buzzing sounded; his system was warning him that it

33

was having difficulty compensating for this sudden adrenaline rush that was unaccompanied by strenuous physical exertion. He drew in several deep breaths to try to calm himself down.

'Tell me – where is he?'

'I don't think so. I've called a halt to the operation,' Wiedermann said offhandedly, frowning at the file in his hands.

'You did what?' Xris couldn't believe he'd heard correctly, thought his auditory system might have shorted out.

'I spoke clearly enough.' Wiedermann was testy. The green eyes narrowed. 'I've halted the operation. I have a good idea – an excellent idea, in fact – where this case is headed. And I don't like it. We could find ourselves in a great deal of difficulty. Our firm is not, at this point, prepared to accept the risk. I've spoken with my father and he – '

With his good hand, Xris shoved aside an enormous stack of folders, toppling them to the floor. He leaned over the desk, planted the left elbow of the metal arm in the newly cleared space directly under Wiedermann's nose.

'You see this?' Xris wiggled his metal fingers. 'Nine years ago, this arm was real. So was my leg, my eye, and all other parts of me. I won't bore you with the details – you've got them on file. I damn near died in that explosion. Dalin Rowan, my friend and partner, saved my life. But I never got a chance to thank him. After the accident, he disappeared.

'I owe him.' Xris was forced to pause, readjust himself. He was experiencing momentary breathing difficulty. 'I owe him big. I spent a year of my own life searching for Dalin Rowan. No luck. You've spent six years' worth of my money searching for him. You tell me you've found him, but you won't tell me where he is. I think you might want to reconsider. Hand over that file.'

'Certainly.' Wiedermann was calm, not the least intimidated. 'But you wouldn't find it much help. It's not your case. Here, see for yourself.'

Xris backed off. He'd played enough ante-up to know when a man was bluffing. 'All right, then. Where are my files?'

'In the computer.' Wiedermann indicated the screens behind him. '*One* of the computers. You'll never find them, you know. Not if you searched a lifetime. And I didn't say I *wouldn't* tell you. I haven't decided.'

'What do you want?' Xris demanded. 'More money?'

Wiedermann shook his head. 'We operate in this galaxy at His Majesty's pleasure. At any time, the galactic government could revoke our license. If that happened, the total worth of the Crown Jewels couldn't compensate us for our losses. If your case results in legal action against us, I want to be certain we have a chance to win.'

'Legal action?' Xris snorted. 'What legal action? I'm trying to find my friend –'

'It's up to you,' Wiedermann interrupted. 'If we decide not to proceed, you won't be charged for our time. We'll refund your retainer. You won't be out anything.'

'Only eight years of my life,' Xris said through clenched teeth.

'Tell me your story.'

'I told you the goddamn story once. Your operative, that is. It's in the blasted files!'

Wiedermann leaned back in his chair. Crossing bony legs over bony knees, he put the tips of his fingers together.

Xris eyed the computer screens. His fingers twitched. He was good with computers, but he wasn't that good. Dalin Rowan – now there had been the computer expert. In all these years, Xris had never run across anyone as good as Dalin.

Slowly, reluctantly, the cyborg sat back down.

Xris paused a moment to get his thoughts in order. It didn't take long. Not a day went by but that he didn't think about it. Wondering, trying to make sense of it.

'It was back during the days of the democracy. I was a Fed, a member of the bureau detailed to handle interplanetary crime. I don't know how much you know about the agency; probably quite a bit.'

Wiedermann smiled, nodded. 'The bureau hasn't changed all that much under the new regime. Cleaned up some, maybe. But basically the same.'

'No reason it should change,' Xris said. 'They've got good people. We were good, most of us. Dedicated. Loyal. And if there *was* some corruption, hell, that's only to be expected in an organization that big. Of course, I didn't know at the time that the whole damn government was corrupt, from the president on down. Not

35

that it would have made much difference, I guess. I did what I did for the bureau for my own reasons.'

'And those were?'

Xris shrugged. Taking out the cigarette case, he held it in his hand, but didn't open it. He tapped it thoughtfully with a good finger.

'It's no big moral thing with me. Right. Wrong. Good. Bad. Ethics vary from planet to planet. On Adonia twenty years ago, it was legal to abandon a child for being ugly. We had a hell of a time with local laws. But that's not important. What got to me, what kept me going, were the people who got fat off other people's misery.'

'Yes, go on.'

Xris shifted in his chair, attempted to make himself more comfortable. Not an easy task when half his body was metal.

'I don't suppose you'd let me smoke?'

Wiedermann shook his head, patted his chest. 'Asthma.'

Xris removed a twist from the case, clamped his teeth down on it, chewed it. The bitter juice flooded his mouth, washed out the faint metallic flavor that he always tasted, despite the fact that the doctors told him it was all in his mind. Some days the taste was stronger than others.

'It's what kept me from being on the take, I guess. I had my chances, but I knew where the money came from: babies who were born whacked out from drugs, sixteen-year-old hookers smashed up by their pimps, old people swindled out of their life savings. These people were at the bottom and at the top were guys in the fancy limojets who held handkerchiefs over their delicate noses when they drove through the stinking slums they helped create. Bringing those guys down, making them lie flat on the pavement in the muck and the filth, rubbing those delicate noses in it – that's why I worked for the bureau.'

Xris thrust the case back in his shirt pocket. 'I had money enough. Everything I needed, everything I wanted. My wife and I –'

Xris stopped abruptly, smiled easily. 'But you don't want to hear all that. It was a long time ago, anyway. And it all came down to one job. One simple, routine job . . .'

4

To unfailingly take what you attack, attack where there is no defense. For unfailingly secure defense, defend where there is no attack.

Sun Tzu, *The Art of War*

Xris and his longtime friend and partner Mashahiro Ito forced their way through the crowds pouring out of the mass transit station, walked the short distance to the main entrance of FISA headquarters. The season was spring on Janus 2. The gardens decorating the grounds were just beginning to come back to life after their winter's hiatus. Budding trees extended protective limbs over the tentatively blooming flower beds. Ito had once discoursed at great length on the symbology of the protective trees, the helpless flowers. Xris, grinning, had once told Ito what he could do with his symbology.

A large and massive sign read ADMINISTRATIVE GOVERNMENT FACILITY, JANUS 2. The sign made no mention of the fact that the Federal Intelligence and Security Agency was housed inside the building; it was supposedly top secret. But everyone on the planet knew. Janus 2 was quite proud of it. The building was a regular stop for tour shuttles.

The agents dodged a group of uniformed schoolchildren, who squealed with delight.

'I'll bet he's a Fed!'

'Hey, mister, can we see your gun?'

Xris shook his head, kept walking. A large and ugly electrified fence – a grim contrast to the flower beds – surrounded the building. Xris was always meaning to ask Ito what symbology the fence held.

'Any idea what this meeting is about?'

'Nope,' Ito answered, lowered his voice. 'But it's bound to be about the Hung. We've been working on this damn case for months now. Word is it's ready to break.'

37

'About time! I hope this isn't another of those goddamn ass-numbing talk sessions. Sit around and yammer at one another for hours and get nothing done.'

Ito laughed, but he wasn't very sympathetic. He liked the planning part of any assignment, considered it a 'cerebral exercise.' Xris considered it bullshit. He liked the action – the forty-four-decawatt lasgun pointing at some punk's skull and the 'Freeze, Federal agents! Hands behind your head!' part of the operation.

'Is Rowan coming?'

'I don't know,' Xris said shortly. 'I haven't seen much of him lately.'

Ito cast a sharp glance at his friend. Xris was aware of the scrutiny, did his best to ignore it. Dalin Rowan was the third member of what a few in the agency jokingly called the Trinity. Xris, Ito, and Rowan: Father, Son, and Holy Ghost, so named because Xris was the oldest and the biggest; Ito was short, slender, and the youngest; Rowan was quiet, unassuming, and could walk through a computer without leaving a trace behind. The three had worked together for years now and were one of the top teams in the agency. They were also close friends. Or rather, they used to be.

The two agents entered the first checkpoint – a small access building with two doors. One door provided entrance through the electrified fence, the other door granted access to the facility. Security guards checked ID badges and issued visitor passes to those who were cleared for them.

The senior guard looked up from his newsvid reader and nodded.

'Going to cause any trouble today, Xris? I just need to know, so's I can plan my lunch break around you.'

Xris shook his head. 'Hell, that was an accident, Henry. I didn't mean to set off the alarms. I forgot I had the damn knife on me.'

'Huh-uh.' Henry grinned. He'd been an agent once, until he could no longer pass the physical. But that had been at age eighty. He still had a grip like a nullgrav steel vise – as Xris had good reason to know.

'You're in charge of him today, Ito. I'm getting too old for this sort of thing.'

'You'll outlive us all, Henry.' Ito laughed.

Xris was to remember that remark.

He and Ito entered the main administration headquarters building, encountered another security guard.

Ito pulled his lasgun out of his shoulder holster and placed it on the counter. 'Morning, boys.' Folding his arms, sighing, he settled back to wait.

Xris laid his regulation lasgun on the counter. He drew forth a small modified derringer from his suit pocket and placed it on the counter. Next came a long, thin blade from the back of his jacket, a needle-gun from a leg holster, and a boot knife.

'Glad you're here to protect us, Father,' Ito said.

'And I always will be, my son,' Xris returned solemnly, and patted Ito on the head.

They walked without incident through the weapons detectors, headed for the lifts.

'Floor thirty-five,' Xris said, and inserted his security card.

The lift whisked them up, stopped. Stepping out, Xris and Ito glanced up at the briefing screen.

'Mission briefing 2122027, 0845hrs, 3506.'

'That's us.'

The two were early for the briefing, but they weren't alone. Another man sat at a desk in the back, sipping coffee and working on a portable computer. He looked up, smiled, nodded. Xris and Ito nodded back, took their seats at the desks that made this room resemble a classroom.

Xris was back up a moment later, going to get coffee for himself, tea for Ito. He'd just returned to his seat when Ito nudged him. Dalin Rowan had walked in.

'Dalin, how's it going?' Ito asked pleasantly.

'Okay,' Rowan replied.

His lips jerked in what was intended for a smile, but didn't quite make it. And nothing sounded less okay than his 'Okay.'

He took a seat in the center of the room, about four chairs removed from Xris and Ito. The stranger in the back had finished his coffee, continued to work on the computer.

'Been a long time, buddy,' Xris said quietly. 'I've been worried about you.' It was an apology.

Rowan glanced up. He was pale, thin, had obviously lost weight. He attempted the jerky pseudo-smile again.

'Sorry I haven't called, Xris. I . . . I've had a lot on my mind lately.' Rowan glanced at the stranger in the back, added, 'I'll talk to you after the meeting.'

Xris nodded, settled back, relieved. He and Rowan had not parted on the best of terms and he hadn't seen or heard from his friend in a month. All because of that damn bitch. Xris had tried to point out to his friend what everyone else knew but was too polite to mention: The whore was taking Rowan for a ride. A wild and thrill-packed ride, maybe, but a ride nonetheless. An expensive ride.

You goddamn fool! You're thinking with your zipper, not your brains! Xris recalled those words clearly. They were the last words said between them.

Rumor had it now that the slut had left Rowan. When he could no longer pay for the tickets, the amusement park had shut down the rides. Looking at his friend, Xris guessed that this time the rumor was true. He wondered uncomfortably if other rumors were true, as well. That Rowan was in big financial trouble, seriously in debt.

Well, Xris reflected, I'll find out soon enough.

The superintendent entered, accompanied by an older woman wearing a flight suit. Xris and Ito exchanged glances. They'd been right. The super was Jafar el Amadi, top man on the Hung Conspiracy case. So that's what this was all about.

The meeting came to order.

Amadi opened with a frown; but then, he always frowned.

'Agents, this briefing will be kept short. First, I'd like to introduce your controller, Agent Michael Armstrong.'

Xris twisted in his desk. The man in the back acknowledged the introduction. Tall, thin, and middle-aged, Armstrong didn't look as if he had the stamina for fieldwork; probably why he was assigned to the more sedentary controller role.

'Next I want to introduce Captain Lisa Bolton, skipper of the *Vigilance*, our new orbital control ship. All right, let's get down to business.

'To sum up: we have reason to believe that the Hung have infiltrated the very top levels of the galactic government. We don't have any hard evidence, but there are several indications, most noteworthy being Senator Gravesborne changing his vote at the last minute on the arms control legislation which went down to defeat last month. Because of this defeat, the Hung were able to start up a munitions plant on TISor 13 and a weapons factory on TISor 8. The syndicate doesn't need these weapons; the Hung are well supplied. Obviously, they're not manufacturing guns for themselves. They're selling them. And now we think we know who's buying – the Corasians.'

Xris sat up straight. Even Rowan, who had been staring listlessly at his desk, lifted his head, his attention caught. The Corasians occupied the galaxy next door and wanted to take over the entire neighborhood. Unfortunately, when the Corasians moved in, they had a bad habit of devouring the neighbors. Made entirely of energy, the fiery bloblike entities roamed about searching for food – any living being would do, but Corasians were particularly fond of human flesh.

'This is only a suspicion, mind you. We can't prove anything – yet. That's why you're all here today. As you can imagine,' the super continued grimly, 'I've got the boss on my back on this one. Chief Superintendent Robison is in my office more than I am lately. President Robes has taken a personal interest in this investigation, ladies and gentlemen, so let's do this one right. I want to retire in four years on schedule. Got it?'

They all nodded. Xris, glancing at Rowan, was pleased to see some color in his friend's wan face. Work – the best remedy for whatever ailed you. Even a broken heart.

'Let's get down to details. Xris, you and Ito and Rowan will conduct a raid on the munitions plant on TISor 13. Word is that's where their central computer system is located. Rowan will handle the computer end. Xris and Ito will find out what's being produced and if it's been designed with those damn Corasian blobs and their robot casings in mind. Once we get hard evidence, we can bust this thing wide open.

'Xris and Ito will land on TISor 13 first, stake out the factory. I've booked passage on the *IJD Lentian* for the two of you, arriving at TISor 4 in seven days. From there, you'll rent a spaceplane and fly to TISor 13.

'Rowan, you'll travel with Armstrong on the *Vigilance*, then

41

link up with Xris and Ito planetside just before the raid. I have no idea what sort of computer equipment these people are running, so bring everything in your tool kit.'

Xris was disappointed that they weren't traveling together. Get Rowan alone for seven days and his two best friends would have him just about back to normal in no time.

'Excuse the interruption, Super,' Xris spoke up. 'But why not send Rowan along with us?'

Amadi was extremely irritated at the interruption. 'We've intercepted some coded transmissions from the Hung. Our computers can't crack them. I want Rowan to work on them and he can do so only with the sophisticated equipment on board the *Vigilance*. I trust this meets with your approval, Agent?'

Xris ignored the sarcasm. The super was under a lot of pressure these days. 'Sure thing, sir.' He looked over at Rowan, who gave him a smile – a real smile.

'Good.' Amadi grunted. 'Now, where was I?' He peered at his notes. 'Armstrong, your post will be on the *Vigilance*. You'll act as onsite mission commander – guide everyone into the factory and out again.

'Now listen to me.' Amadi rested both hands on the desk, leaned over it. 'I don't need to tell you how vital this mission is. Everything must go according to plan. Yes, I'm talking to you, Xris. You listen to the controller on this one and do exactly what he says or so help me you'll be back on Jackson's Moon busting cyberpunkers. Understood?'

Xris caught Ito's wink and swallowed the retort that would have only landed him in trouble. There wasn't much he could say in his own defense. He'd been right in ignoring the controller's warnings two times out of three, but it was the third – when he'd been wrong – that had nearly gotten them all killed. It was also the reason they now had a new controller. Xris heard that Polinskai had taken early retirement. He nodded glumly.

The super turned. 'Captain Bolton, how soon will your ship be ready to leave?'

'Six days, sir. We've just finished ship's run-up trials, and need to take on all provisions and load the system's computers with the operational data for this mission.'

'Very well, then, Captain. Six days it is. Armstrong, you and

Rowan coordinate with the captain here for all transport details. You will establish contact with Xris and Ito on TISor 13 at oh-two hundred hours on the ninth. Rowan, you'll get a chance to fly one of the *Vigilance*'s new intrusion shuttles. You'll meet up with Xris and Ito on the surface, and Agent Armstrong will guide you in from his post on *Vigilance*. Anything else?'

Armstrong raised his hand. 'I'd like to run over the details of the plan with the other agents after this, if that's convenient with them.'

The super glanced around. The others shrugged, agreed.

'If there's nothing else, good luck!' Amadi dismissed the meeting.

Everyone stood as the superintendent and Captain Bolton left. When they were gone, Ito walked over to their new controller, held out his hand.

'Mashahiro Ito. I haven't met you before. Are you new in the agency?'

Armstrong shook hands. 'No. I've been in for a few years now, working out of Central Headquarters. My specialization is the Corasians. I've been acting as our liaison with Naval Intelligence. I was due a change, so I requested a field assignment. They figured I could be useful on this case.'

'Fed up with the politics, huh?' Xris was sympathetic. He, too, shook hands. 'Name's Xris.'

'No one can pronounce his surname, so we just skip it,' Ito added.

For a man with not much muscle tone, Armstrong's handshake was surprisingly firm and strong. 'Life in the capital *is* pretty stressful,' he said in answer to Xris's question.

And that, thought Xris, is all we'll hear about HQ. For a while, at least. Though Armstrong doesn't look the type to open up. Pity. It'd be nice to know if the word floating around about disorganization and turmoil at the top is true.

Rowan shook hands with their new controller, mumbled 'Nice to meet you,' then asked abruptly, 'What time's the briefing?'

Armstrong blinked and answered, 'Twenty-two hundred, if that's okay with everyone? I thought – '

'Fine.'

Rowan left, moving so rapidly that Xris fell over a desk in his effort to catch up. He caught his friend at the door.

'Hey, buddy, I thought we were going to talk. Look, I've got an idea. Come home with me to dinner. We've got six hours before the briefing with Armstrong. Marjorie's cooking something special – one of her famous "welcome home" meals. She'd love to see you. She said she didn't hear from you the whole time I was away. You know how she worries . . .'

Rowan was shaking his head, doing his best to escape out the door. But Xris was a big man, broad-shouldered and tall, and made a sizable obstacle.

His attempt foiled, Rowan halted, stared impatiently past his friend into the hall. 'Thanks, Xris, but I just remembered an appointment – '

'Cancel it.'

Rowan shook his head. 'I'm afraid that's not possible. I'll see you at the briefing.'

He tried to step around. Xris grabbed hold of his friend's arm. 'Goddammit, Dalin, I'm sorry – '

Rowan looked directly at Xris for the first time since he'd entered the room.

'For what?' Rowan asked bitterly. 'Being right?'

Slender, shorter than Xris, Dalin Rowan was wiry and agile. He feinted left, moved right, and was out the door before Xris could stop him.

'No luck?' said Ito, coming up behind.

'Hell no. He's acting strange, Ito. He could be in trouble. Big trouble. I heard – '

'Excuse me,' Armstrong interrupted politely. He was standing behind them. 'If I could get past? I need to put together a few things.'

'Sure. Sorry.' Xris moved one way, Ito the other.

Armstrong stepped between them, gave them a smile, and walked off down the hall.

'What have you heard?' Ito asked.

'Nothing,' Xris answered. 'Skip it.'

Ito shook his head. 'You heard he was on the take. I heard it, too, and I don't believe it.'

'I *didn't*. Until I saw him.'

44

'Rowan's a straight arrow. You'll never convince me.'

They both stood in the doorway, watched their friend step into the lift.

Xris took out a twist, stuck it in his mouth, chewed on the end. 'Maybe one of us should . . . well . . . keep an eye on him.'

'Damn it, Xris, we're talking about Rowan! Dalin Rowan!' Ito snorted. 'If you want to tail a man who's been your best friend for ten years, who's saved your ass more than once, then go ahead. I'm going out for a drink. You coming?'

Xris went with Ito for that drink. But he was to wonder later — wonder over and over again – what would have happened if he hadn't. What if he'd tailed his friend, his pal, his buddy? What would he have seen? Rowan meeting with the Hung. Taking their filthy blood money. Selling his friends out.

Why? Why the hell didn't I go after him? Xris was to ask himself that question during the long, pain-tormented nights. And he always came up with the same answer.

Because he was my friend. A man doesn't tail his best friend.

But then neither does a man set his best friends up for the kill.

_____ already in the briefing room when Xris entered. _____ _____ments, Ito wandered in, glanced worriedly at Xris, who had been moody and morose in the bar.

Xris smiled, nodded, indicated that he was once more in his right senses. An excellent meal – all his favorite food – and Marjorie's reassuring, levelheaded conversation had eased his mind. Dalin hadn't sold anyone out. He'd be fine. Some things a man had to work out on his own.

Ito grinned, relieved. He began to examine a map of TISor 13 that Armstrong had brought up on the large vidscreen.

Dalin came in, sat down next to Xris.

'I'm sorry,' Rowan said abruptly. 'But everything's going to be okay now. It's all . . . taken care of.'

'What is? Look, Dalin, if you need cash, I've got a few extra credits in my account –'

'No, no,' Rowan said hastily, with a bleak smile. 'It's all

arranged. I can't explain now. When this job's done, I'm going to be all right. I promise, Xris. Don't worry. It's going to be all right.'

He looked at Xris anxiously, either begging him to drop the subject or desperately eager to talk. Xris couldn't tell which, and whatever he might have said in return never got said because at that moment Armstrong started talking.

Turning to the wall-mounted vidscreen, he called up a map of the munitions factory and surrounding areas.

'I've prepared some briefing notes; you can go over them at your convenience. I'll cover everything first, and then you can ask questions.'

Using a red-light laser indicator, Armstrong pointed out a gray area near the munitions plant. 'You'll make your approach from here. This swamp is the only easy point of access. The water and assorted plant life provide excellent cover right up to within three meters of the fence that surrounds the facility.'

'Swamp!' Ito repeated, horrified. 'Assorted plant life! What does that mean? And what about assorted animal life?'

Armstrong was soothing. 'I've checked it out. According to our biometeorological research scientists, there's nothing too danger-ous in the swamp.'

'How the hell do they know?'

'No, but studies on swamps on planets with the same type of atmosphere and temperature would seem to indicate that the flora is standard for warm, wet environments. Nothing worse than skunk plants and plenty of vines. They don't think any of the vines are sentient.'

'Don't *think* they're sentient,' Xris kidded, nudging Ito under the table with his foot.

Ito paled.

'You shouldn't have to worry about the fauna, either,' Armstrong continued. 'Primarily your standard water lizards and tubor snakes and they don't like anything bigger than they are.'

'Snakes . . .' Ito repeated in a whisper.

'Tubor snakes. Not poisonous. You'll be provided with the standard snakebite kit, just in case. To continue' – Armstrong hastened on, ignoring Ito's garbled protest – 'you'll enter the swamp here and move to this point, closest to the fence. You'll

46

'Rowan's a straight arrow. You'll never convince me.'

They both stood in the doorway, watched their friend step into the lift.

Xris took out a twist, stuck it in his mouth, chewed on the end. 'Maybe one of us should . . . well . . . keep an eye on him.'

'Damn it, Xris, we're talking about Rowan! Dalin Rowan!' Ito snorted. 'If you want to tail a man who's been your best friend for ten years, who's saved your ass more than once, then go ahead. I'm going out for a drink. You coming?'

Xris went with Ito for that drink. But he was to wonder later – wonder over and over again – what would have happened if he hadn't. What if he'd tailed his friend, his pal, his buddy? What would he have seen? Rowan meeting with the Hung. Taking their filthy blood money. Selling his friends out.

Why? Why the hell didn't I go after him? Xris was to ask himself that question during the long, pain-tormented nights. And he always came up with the same answer.

Because he was my friend. A man doesn't tail his best friend.

But then neither does a man set his best friends up for the kill.

Armstrong was already in the briefing room when Xris entered. He sat down and waited. After a few moments, Ito wandered in, glanced worriedly at Xris, who had been moody and morose in the bar.

Xris smiled, nodded, indicated that he was once more in his right senses. An excellent meal – all his favorite food – and Marjorie's reassuring, levelheaded conversation had eased his mind. Dalin hadn't sold anyone out. He'd be fine. Some things a man had to work out on his own.

Ito grinned, relieved. He began to examine a map of TISor 13 that Armstrong had brought up on the large vidscreen.

Dalin came in, sat down next to Xris.

'I'm sorry,' Rowan said abruptly. 'But everything's going to be okay now. It's all . . . taken care of.'

'What is? Look, Dalin, if you need cash, I've got a few extra credits in my account –'

'No, no,' Rowan said hastily, with a bleak smile. 'It's all

45

arranged. I can't explain now. When this job's done, I'm going to be all right. I promise, Xris. Don't worry. It's going to be all right.'

He looked at Xris anxiously, either begging him to drop the subject or desperately eager to talk. Xris couldn't tell which, and whatever he might have said in return never got said because at that moment Armstrong started talking.

Turning to the wall-mounted vidscreen, he called up a map of the munitions factory and surrounding areas.

'I've prepared some briefing notes; you can go over them at your convenience. I'll cover everything first, and then you can ask questions.'

Using a red-light laser indicator, Armstrong pointed out a gray area near the munitions plant. 'You'll make your approach from here. This swamp is the only easy point of access. The water and assorted plant life provide excellent cover right up to within three meters of the fence that surrounds the facility.'

'Swamp!' Ito repeated, horrified. 'Assorted plant life! What does that mean? And what about assorted animal life?'

Armstrong was soothing. 'I've checked it out. According to our biometeorological research scientists, there's nothing too dangerous in the swamp.'

'How the hell do they know? Have they been there?'

'No, but studies on swamps on planets with the same type of atmosphere and temperature would seem to indicate that the flora is standard for warm, wet environments. Nothing worse than skunk plants and plenty of vines. They don't think any of the vines are sentient.'

'Don't *think* they're sentient,' Xris kidded, nudging Ito under the table with his foot.

Ito paled.

'You shouldn't have to worry about the fauna, either,' Armstrong continued. 'Primarily your standard water lizards and tubor snakes and they don't like anything bigger than they are.'

'Snakes . . .' Ito repeated in a whisper.

'Tubor snakes. Not poisonous. You'll be provided with the standard snakebite kit, just in case. To continue' – Armstrong hastened on, ignoring Ito's garbled protest – 'you'll enter the swamp here and move to this point, closest to the fence. You'll

46